THE DEATH OF THE LION

By HENRY JAMES

Index Of Contents
The Death of the Lion
Henry James – A Biography

The Death of the Lion

Chapter I

I HAD simply, I suppose, a change of heart, and it must have begun when I received my manuscript back from Mr. Pinhorn. Mr. Pinhorn was my "chief," as he was called in the office: he had the high mission of bringing the paper up. This was a weekly periodical, which had been supposed to be almost past redemption when he took hold of it. It was Mr. Deedy who had let the thing down so dreadfully: he was never mentioned in the office now save in connexion with that misdemeanour. Young as I was I had been in a manner taken over from Mr. Deedy, who had been owner as well as editor; forming part of a promiscuous lot, mainly plant and office-furniture, which poor Mrs. Deedy, in her bereavement and depression, parted with at a rough valuation. I could account for my continuity but on the supposition that I had been cheap. I rather resented the practice of fathering all flatness on my late protector, who was in his unhonoured grave; but as I had my way to make I found matter enough for complacency in being on a "staff." At the same time I was aware of my exposure to suspicion as a product of the old lowering system. This made me feel I was doubly bound to have ideas, and had doubtless been at the bottom of my proposing to Mr. Pinhorn that I should lay my lean hands on Neil Paraday. I remember how he looked at me - quite, to begin with, as if he had never heard of this celebrity, who indeed at that moment was by no means in the centre of the heavens; and even when I had knowingly explained he expressed but little confidence in the demand for any such stuff. When I had reminded him that the great principle on which we were supposed to work was just to create the demand we required, he considered a moment and then returned: "I see - you want to write him up."

"Call it that if you like."

"And what's your inducement?"

"Bless my soul - my admiration!"

Mr. Pinhorn pursed up his mouth. "Is there much to be done with him?"

"Whatever there is we should have it all to ourselves, for he hasn't been touched."

This argument was effective and Mr. Pinhorn responded. "Very well, touch him." Then he added: "But where can you do it?"

"Under the fifth rib!"

Mr. Pinhorn stared. "Where's that?"

"You want me to go down and see him?" I asked when I had enjoyed his visible search for the obscure suburb I seemed to have named.

"I don't 'want' anything - the proposal's your own. But you must remember that that's the way we do things NOW," said Mr. Pinhorn with another dig Mr. Deedy.

Unregenerate as I was I could read the queer implications of this speech. The present owner's superior virtue as well as his deeper craft spoke in his reference to the late editor as one of that baser sort who deal in false representations. Mr. Deedy would as soon have sent me to call on Neil Paraday as he would have published a "holiday-number"; but such scruples presented themselves as mere ignoble thrift to his successor, whose own sincerity took the form of ringing door-bells and whose definition of genius was the art of finding people at home. It was as if Mr. Deedy had published reports without his young men's having, as Pinhorn would have said, really been there. I was unregenerate, as I have hinted, and couldn't be concerned to straighten out the journalistic morals of my chief, feeling them indeed to be an abyss over the edge of which it was better not to peer. Really to be there this time moreover was a vision that made the idea of writing something subtle about Neil Paraday only the more inspiring. I would be as considerate as even Mr. Deedy could have wished, and yet I should be as present as only Mr. Pinhorn could conceive. My allusion to the sequestered manner in which Mr. Paraday lived - it had formed part of my explanation, though I knew of it only by hearsay - was, I could divine, very much what had made Mr. Pinhorn nibble. It struck him as inconsistent with the success of his paper that any one should be so sequestered as that. And then wasn't an immediate exposure of everything just what the public wanted? Mr. Pinhorn effectually called me to order by reminding me of the promptness with which I had met Miss Braby at Liverpool on her return from her fiasco in the States. Hadn't we published, while its freshness and flavour were unimpaired, Miss Braby's own version of that great international episode? I felt somewhat uneasy at this lumping of the actress and the author, and I confess that after having enlisted Mr. Pinhorn's sympathies I procrastinated a little. I had succeeded better than I wished, and I had, as it happened, work nearer at hand. A few days later I called on Lord Crouchley and carried off in triumph the most unintelligible statement that had yet appeared of his lordship's reasons for his change of front. I thus set in motion in the daily papers columns of virtuous verbiage. The following week I ran down to Brighton for a chat, as Mr. Pinhorn called it, with Mrs. Bounder, who gave me, on the subject of her divorce, many curious particulars that had not been articulated in court. If ever an article flowed from the primal fount it was that article on Mrs. Bounder. By this time, however, I became aware that Neil Paraday's new book was on the point of appearing and that its approach had been the ground of my original appeal to Mr. Pinhorn, who was now annoyed with me for having lost so many days. He bundled me off - we would at least not lose another. I've always thought his sudden alertness a remarkable example of the journalistic instinct. Nothing had occurred, since I first spoke to him, to create a visible urgency, and no enlightenment could possibly have reached him. It was a pure case of profession flair - he had smelt the coming glory as an animal smells its distant prey.

Chapter II

I MAY as well say at once that this little record pretends in no degree to be a picture either of my introduction to Mr. Paraday or of certain proximate steps and stages. The scheme of my narrative allows no space for these things, and in any case a prohibitory sentiment would hang about my recollection of so rare an hour. These meagre notes are essentially private, so that if they see the light the insidious forces that, as my story itself shows, make at present for publicity will simply have overmastered my precautions. The curtain fell lately enough on the lamentable drama. My memory of the day I alighted at Mr. Paraday's door is a fresh memory of kindness, hospitality, compassion, and of the wonderful illuminating talk in which the welcome was conveyed. Some voice of the air had taught me the right moment, the moment of his life at which an act of unexpected young allegiance might most come home to him. He had recently recovered from a long, grave illness. I had gone to the neighbouring inn for the night, but I spent the evening in his company, and he insisted the next day on my sleeping under his roof. I hadn't an indefinite leave: Mr. Pinhorn supposed us to put our victims through on the gallop. It was later, in the office, that the rude motions of the jig were set to music. I fortified myself, however, as my training had taught me to do, by the conviction that nothing could be more advantageous for my article than to be written in the very atmosphere. I said nothing to Mr. Paraday about it, but in the morning, after my remove from the inn, while he was occupied in his study, as he had notified me he should need to be, I committed to paper the main heads of my impression. Then thinking to commend myself to Mr. Pinhorn by my celerity, I walked out and posted my little packet before luncheon. Once my paper was written I was free to stay on, and if it was calculated to divert attention from my levity in so doing I could reflect with satisfaction that I had never been so clever. I don't mean to deny of course that I was aware it was much too good for Mr. Pinhorn; but I was equally conscious that Mr. Pinhorn had the supreme shrewdness of recognising from time to time the cases in which an article was not too bad only because it was too good. There was nothing he loved so much as to print on the right occasion a thing he hated. I had begun my visit to the great man on a Monday, and on the Wednesday his book came out. A copy of it arrived by the first post, and he let me go out into the garden with it immediately after breakfast, I read it from beginning to end that day, and in the evening he asked me to remain with him the rest of the week and over the Sunday.

That night my manuscript came back from Mr. Pinhorn, accompanied with a letter the gist of which was the desire to know what I meant by trying to fob off on him such stuff. That was the meaning of the question, if not exactly its form, and it made my mistake immense to me. Such as this mistake was I could now only look it in the face and accept it. I knew where I had failed, but it was exactly where I couldn't have succeeded. I had been sent down to be personal and then in point of fact hadn't been personal at all: what I had dispatched to London was just a little finicking feverish study of my author's talent. Anything less relevant to Mr. Pinhorn's purpose couldn't well be imagined, and he was visibly angry at my having (at his expense, with a second-class ticket) approached the subject of our enterprise only to stand off so helplessly. For myself, I knew but too well what had happened, and how a miracle - as pretty as some old miracle of legend - had been wrought on the spot to save me. There had been a big brush of wings, the flash of an opaline robe, and then, with a great cool stir of the air, the sense of an angel's having swooped down and caught me to his bosom. He held me only till the danger was over, and it all took place in a minute. With my manuscript back on my hands I understood the phenomenon better, and the reflexions I made on it are what I meant, at the beginning of this anecdote, by my change of heart. Mr. Pinhorn's note was not only a rebuke decidedly stern, but an invitation immediately to send him - it was the case to say so - the genuine article, the revealing and reverberating sketch to the promise of which, and of which alone, I owed my squandered privilege. A week or two later I recast my peccant paper and, giving it a particular application to Mr. Paraday's new book, obtained for it the hospitality of another journal, where, I must admit, Mr. Pinhorn was so far vindicated as that it attracted not the least attention.

Chapter III

I WAS frankly, at the end of three days, a very prejudiced critic, so that one morning when, in the garden, my great man had offered to read me something I quite held my breath as I listened. It was the written scheme of another book - something put aside long ago, before his illness, but that he had lately taken out again to reconsider. He had been turning it round when I came down on him, and it had grown magnificently under this second hand. Loose liberal confident, it might have passed for a great gossiping eloquent letter - the overflow into talk of an artist's amorous plan. The theme I thought singularly rich, quite the strongest he had yet treated; and this familiar statement of it, full too of fine maturities, was really, in summarised splendour, a mine of gold, a precious independent work. I remember rather profanely wondering whether the ultimate production could possibly keep at the pitch. His reading of the fond epistle, at any rate, made me feel as if I were, for the advantage of posterity, in close correspondence with him - were the distinguished person to whom it had been affectionately addressed. It was a high distinction simply to be told such things. The idea he now communicated had all the freshness, the flushed fairness, of the conception untouched and untried: it was Venus rising from the sea and before the airs had blown upon her. I had never been so throbbingly present at such an unveiling. But when he had tossed the last bright word after the others, as I had seen cashiers in banks, weighing mounds of coin, drop a final sovereign into the tray, I knew a sudden prudent alarm.

"My dear master, how, after all, are you going to do it? It's infinitely noble, but what time it will take, what patience and independence, what assured, what perfect conditions! Oh for a lone isle in a tepid sea!"

"Isn't this practically a lone isle, and aren't you, as an encircling medium, tepid enough?" he asked, alluding with a laugh to the wonder of my young admiration and the narrow limits of his little provincial home. "Time isn't what I've lacked hitherto: the question hasn't been to find it, but to use it. Of course my illness made, while it lasted, a great hole - but I dare say there would have been a hole at any rate. The earth we tread has more pockets than a billiard-table. The great thing is now to keep on my feet."

"That's exactly what I mean."

Neil Paraday looked at me with eyes - such pleasant eyes as he had - in which, as I now recall their expression, I seem to have seen a dim imagination of his fate. He was fifty years old, and his illness had been cruel, his convalescence slow. "It isn't as if I weren't all right."

"Oh if you weren't all right I wouldn't look at you!" I tenderly said.

We had both got up, quickened as by this clearer air, and he had lighted a cigarette. I had taken a fresh one, which with an intenser smile, by way of answer to my exclamation, he applied to the flame of his match. "If I weren't better I shouldn't have thought of THAT!" He flourished his script in his hand.

"I don't want to be discouraging, but that's not true," I returned. "I'm sure that during the months you lay here in pain you had visitations sublime. You thought of a thousand things. You think of more and more all the while. That's what makes you, if you'll pardon my familiarity, so respectable. At a time when so many people are spent you come into your second wind. But, thank God, all the same, you're better! Thank God, too, you're not, as you were telling me yesterday, 'successful.' If YOU weren't a failure what would be the use of trying? That's my one reserve on the subject of your recovery - that it makes you 'score,' as the newspapers say. It looks well in the newspapers, and almost anything that does that's horrible. 'We are happy to announce that Mr. Paraday, the celebrated author, is again in the enjoyment of excellent health.' Somehow I shouldn't like to see it."

"You won't see it; I'm not in the least celebrated - my obscurity protects me. But couldn't you bear even to see I was dying or dead?" my host enquired.

"Dead - passe encore; there's nothing so safe. One never knows what a living artist may do - one has mourned so many. However, one must make the worst of it. You must be as dead as you can."

"Don't I meet that condition in having just published a book?"

"Adequately, let us hope; for the book's verily a masterpiece."

At this moment the parlour-maid appeared in the door that opened from the garden: Paraday lived at no great cost, and the frisk of petticoats, with a timorous "Sherry, sir?" was about his modest mahogany. He allowed half his income to his wife, from whom he had succeeded in separating without redundancy of legend. I had a general faith in his having behaved well, and I had once, in London, taken Mrs. Paraday down to dinner. He now turned to speak to the maid, who offered him, on a tray, some card or note, while, agitated, excited, I wandered to the end of the precinct. The idea of his security became supremely dear to me, and I asked myself if I were the same young man who had come down a few days before to scatter him to the four winds. When I retraced my steps he had gone into the house, and the woman - the second London post had come in - had placed my letters and a newspaper on a bench. I sat down there to the letters, which were a brief business, and then, without heeding the address, took the paper from its envelope. It was the journal of highest renown, THE EMPIRE of that morning. It regularly came to Paraday, but I remembered that neither of us had yet looked at the copy already delivered. This one had a great mark on the "editorial" page, and, uncrumpling the wrapper, I saw it to be directed to my host and stamped with the name of his publishers. I instantly divined that THE EMPIRE had spoken of him, and I've not forgotten the odd little shock of the circumstance. It checked all eagerness and made me drop the paper a moment. As I sat there conscious of a palpitation I think I had a vision of what was to be. I had also a vision of the letter I would presently address to Mr. Pinhorn, breaking, as it were, with Mr. Pinhorn. Of course, however, the next minute the voice of THE EMPIRE was in my ears.

The article wasn't, I thanked heaven, a review; it was a "leader," the last of three, presenting Neil Paraday to the human race. His new book, the fifth from his hand, had been but a day or two out, and THE EMPIRE, already aware of it, fired, as if on the birth of a prince, a salute of a whole column. The guns had been booming these three hours in the house without our suspecting them. The big blundering newspaper had discovered him, and now he was proclaimed and anointed and crowned. His place was assigned him as publicly as if a fat usher with a wand had pointed to the topmost chair; he was to pass up and still up, higher and higher, between the watching faces and the envious sounds - away up to the dais and the throne. The article was "epoch-making," a landmark in his life; he had taken rank at a bound, waked up a national glory. A national glory was needed, and it was an immense convenience he was there. What all this meant rolled over me, and I fear I grew a little faint - it meant so much more than I could say "yea" to on the spot. In a flash, somehow, all was different; the tremendous wave I speak of had swept something away. It had knocked down, I suppose, my little customary altar, my twinkling tapers and my flowers, and had reared itself into the likeness of a temple vast and bare. When Neil Paraday should come out of the house he would come out a contemporary. That was what had happened: the poor man was to be squeezed into his horrible age. I felt as if he had been overtaken on the crest of the hill and brought back to the city. A little more and he would have dipped down the short cut to posterity and escaped.

Chapter IV

WHEN he came out it was exactly as if he had been in custody, for beside him walked a stout man with a big black beard, who, save that he wore spectacles, might have been a policeman, and in whom at a second glance I recognised the highest contemporary enterprise.

"This is Mr. Morrow," said Paraday, looking, I thought, rather white: "he wants to publish heaven knows what about me."

I winced as I remembered that this was exactly what I myself had wanted. "Already?" I cried with a sort of sense that my friend had fled to me for protection.

Mr. Morrow glared, agreeably, through his glasses: they suggested the electric headlights of some monstrous modem ship, and I felt as if Paraday and I were tossing terrified under his bows. I saw his momentum was irresistible. "I was confident that I should be the first in the field. A great interest is naturally felt in Mr. Paraday's surroundings," he heavily observed.

"I hadn't the least idea of it," said Paraday, as if he had been told he had been snoring.

"I find he hasn't read the article in THE EMPIRE," Mr. Morrow remarked to me. "That's so very interesting - it's something to start with," he smiled. He had begun to pull off his gloves, which were violently new, and to look encouragingly round the little garden. As a "surrounding" I felt how I myself had already been taken in; I was a little fish in the stomach of a bigger one. "I represent," our visitor continued, "a syndicate of influential journals, no less than thirty-seven, whose public - whose publics, I may say - are in peculiar sympathy with Mr. Paraday's line of thought. They would greatly appreciate any expression of his views on the subject of the art he so nobly exemplifies. In addition to my connexion with the syndicate just mentioned I hold a particular commission from THE TATLER, whose most prominent department, 'Smatter and Chatter' - I dare say you've often enjoyed it - attracts such attention. I was honoured only last week, as a representative of THE TATLER, with the confidence of Guy Walsingham, the brilliant author of 'Obsessions.' She pronounced herself thoroughly pleased with my sketch of her method; she went so far as to say that I had made her genius more comprehensible even to herself."

Neil Paraday had dropped on the garden-bench and sat there at once detached and confounded; he looked hard at a bare spot in the lawn, as if with an anxiety that had suddenly made him grave. His movement had been interpreted by his visitor as an invitation to sink sympathetically into a wicker chair that stood hard by, and while Mr. Morrow so settled himself I felt he had taken official possession and that there was no undoing it. One had heard of unfortunate people's having "a man in the house," and this was just what we had. There was a silence of a moment, during which we seemed to acknowledge in the only way that was possible the presence of universal fate; the sunny stillness took no pity, and my thought, as I was sure Paraday's was doing, performed within the minute a great distant revolution. I saw just how emphatic I should make my rejoinder to Mr. Pinhorn, and that having come, like Mr. Morrow, to betray, I must remain as long as possible to save. Not because I had brought my mind back, but because our visitors last words were in my ear, I presently enquired with gloomy irrelevance if Guy Walsingham were a woman.

"Oh yes, a mere pseudonym - rather pretty, isn't it? - and convenient, you know, for a lady who goes in for the larger latitude. 'Obsessions, by Miss So-and-so,' would look a little odd, but men are more naturally indelicate. Have you peeped into 'Obsessions'?" Mr. Morrow continued sociably to our companion.

Paraday, still absent, remote, made no answer, as if he hadn't heard the question: a form of intercourse that appeared to suit the cheerful Mr. Morrow as well as any other. Imperturbably bland, he was a man of resources - he only needed to be on the spot. He had pocketed the whole poor place while Paraday and I were wool-gathering, and I could imagine that he had already got his "heads." His system, at any rate, was justified by the inevitability with which I replied, to save my friend the trouble: "Dear no - he hasn't read it. He doesn't read such things!" I unwarily added.

"Things that are TOO far over the fence, eh?" I was indeed a godsend to Mr. Morrow. It was the psychological moment; it determined the appearance of his note-book, which, however, he at first kept slightly behind him, even as the dentist approaching his victim keeps the horrible forceps. "Mr. Paraday holds with the good old proprieties - I see!" And thinking of the thirty-seven influential journals, I found myself, as I found poor Paraday, helplessly assisting at the promulgation of this ineptitude. "There's no point on which distinguished views are so acceptable as on this question - raised perhaps more strikingly than ever by Guy Walsingham - of the permissibility of the larger latitude. I've an appointment, precisely in connexion with it, next week, with Dora Forbes, author of 'The Other Way Round,' which everybody's talking about. Has Mr. Paraday glanced at 'The Other Way Round'?" Mr. Morrow now frankly appealed to me. I took on myself to repudiate the supposition, while our companion, still silent, got up nervously and walked away. His visitor paid no heed to his withdrawal; but opened out the note-book with a more fatherly pat. "Dora Forbes, I gather, takes the ground, the same as Guy Walsingham's, that the larger latitude has simply got to come. He holds that it has got to be squarely faced. Of course his sex makes him a less prejudiced witness. But an authoritative word from Mr. Paraday - from the point of view of HIS sex, you know - would go right round the globe. He takes the line that we HAVEN'T got to face it?"

I was bewildered: it sounded somehow as if there were three sexes. My interlocutor's pencil was poised, my private responsibility great. I simply sat staring, none the less, and only found presence of mind to say: "Is this Miss Forbes a gentleman?"

Mr. Morrow had a subtle smile. "It wouldn't be 'Miss' - there's a wife!"

"I mean is she a man?"

"The wife?" - Mr. Morrow was for a moment as confused as myself. But when I explained that I alluded to Dora Forbes in person he informed me, with visible amusement at my being so out of it, that this was the "pen-name" of an indubitable male - he had a big red moustache. "He goes in for the slight mystification because the ladies are such popular favourites. A great deal of interest is felt in his acting on that idea - which IS clever, isn't it? - and there's every prospect of its being widely imitated." Our host at this moment joined us again, and Mr. Morrow remarked invitingly that he should be happy to make a note of any observation the movement in question, the bid for success under a lady's name, might suggest to Mr. Paraday. But the poor man, without catching the allusion, excused himself, pleading that, though greatly honoured by his visitor's interest, he suddenly felt unwell and should have to take leave of him - have to go and lie down and keep quiet. His young friend might be trusted to answer for him, but he hoped Mr. Morrow didn't expect great things even of his young friend. His young friend, at this moment, looked at Neil Paraday with an anxious eye, greatly wondering if he were doomed to be ill again; but Paraday's own kind face met his question reassuringly, seemed to say in a glance intelligible enough: "Oh I'm not ill, but I'm scared; get him out of the house as quietly as possible." Getting newspaper-men out of the house was odd business for an emissary of Mr. Pinhorn, and I was so exhilarated by the idea of it that I called after him as he left us: "Read the article in THE EMPIRE and you'll soon be all right!"

Chapter V

"DELICIOUS my having come down to tell him of it!" Mr. Morrow ejaculated. "My cab was at the door twenty minutes after THE EMPIRE had been laid on my breakfast-table. Now what have you got for me?" he continued, dropping again into his chair, from which, however, he the next moment eagerly rose. "I was shown into the drawing-room, but there must be more to see - his study, his literary sanctum, the little things he has about, or other domestic objects and features. He wouldn't be lying down on his study-table? There's a great interest always felt in the scene of an author's labours. Sometimes we're favoured with very delightful peeps. Dora Forbes showed me all his table-drawers, and almost jammed my hand into one into which I made a dash! I don't ask that of you, but if we could talk things over right there where he sits I feel as if I should get the keynote."

I had no wish whatever to be rude to Mr. Morrow, I was much too initiated not to tend to more diplomacy; but I had a quick inspiration, and I entertained an insurmountable, an almost superstitious objection to his crossing the threshold of my friend's little lonely shabby consecrated workshop. "No, no - we shan't get at his life that way," I said. "The way to get at his life is to - But wait a moment!" I broke off and went quickly into the house, whence I in three minutes reappeared before Mr. Morrow with the two volumes of Paraday's new book. "His life's here," I went on, "and I'm so full of this admirable thing that I can't talk of anything else. The artist's life's his work, and this is the place to observe him. What he has to tell us he tells us with THIS perfection. My dear sir, the best interviewer is the best reader."

Mr. Morrow good-humouredly protested. "Do you mean to say that no other source of information should be open to us?"

"None other till this particular one - by far the most copious - has been quite exhausted. Have you exhausted it, my dear sir? Had you exhausted it when you came down here? It seems to me in our time almost wholly neglected, and something should surely be done to restore its ruined credit. It's the course to which the artist himself at every step, and with such pathetic confidence, refers us. This last book of Mr. Paraday's is full of revelations."

"Revelations?" panted Mr. Morrow, whom I had forced again into his chair.

"The only kind that count. It tells you with a perfection that seems to me quite final all the author thinks, for instance, about the advent of the 'larger latitude.'"

"Where does it do that?" asked Mr. Morrow, who had picked up the second volume and was insincerely thumbing it.

"Everywhere - in the whole treatment of his case. Extract the opinion, disengage the answer - those are the real acts of homage."

Mr. Morrow, after a minute, tossed the book away. "Ah but you mustn't take me for a reviewer."

"Heaven forbid I should take you for anything so dreadful! You came down to perform a little act of sympathy, and so, I may confide to you, did I. Let us perform our little act together. These pages overflow with the testimony we want: let us read them and taste them and interpret them. You'll of course have perceived for yourself that one scarcely does read Neil Paraday till one reads him aloud; he gives out to the ear an extraordinary full tone, and it's only when you expose it confidently to that test that you really get near his style. Take up your book again and let me listen, while you pay it out, to that wonderful fifteenth chapter. If you feel you can't do it justice, compose yourself to attention while I produce for you - I think I can! - this scarcely less admirable ninth."

Mr. Morrow gave me a straight look which was as hard as a blow between the eyes; he had turned rather red, and a question had formed itself in his mind which reached my sense as distinctly as if he had uttered it: "What sort of a damned fool are YOU?" Then he got up, gathering together his hat and gloves, buttoning his coat, projecting hungrily all over the place the big transparency of his mask. It seemed to flare over Fleet Street and somehow made the actual spot distressingly humble: there was so little for it to feed on unless he counted the blisters of our stucco or saw his way to do something with the roses. Even the poor roses were common kinds. Presently his eyes fell on the manuscript from which Paraday had been reading to me and which still lay on the bench. As my own followed them I saw it looked promising, looked pregnant, as if it gently throbbed with the life the reader had given it. Mr. Morrow indulged in a nod at it and a vague thrust of his umbrella. "What's that?"

"Oh, it's a plan - a secret."

"A secret!" There was an instant's silence, and then Mr. Morrow made another movement. I may have been mistaken, but it affected me as the translated impulse of the desire to lay hands on the manuscript, and this led me to indulge in a quick anticipatory grab which may very well have seemed ungraceful, or even impertinent, and which at any rate left Mr. Paraday's two admirers very erect, glaring at each other while one of them held a bundle of papers well behind him. An instant later Mr. Morrow quitted me abruptly, as if he had really carried something off with him. To reassure myself, watching his broad back recede, I only grasped my manuscript the tighter. He went to the back door of the house, the one he had come out from, but on trying the handle he appeared to find it fastened. So he passed round into the front garden, and by listening intently enough I could presently hear the outer gate close behind him with a bang. I thought again of the thirty-seven influential journals and wondered what would be his revenge. I hasten to add that he was magnanimous: which was just the most dreadful thing he could have been. THE TATLER published a charming chatty familiar account of Mr. Paraday's "Home-life," and on the wings of the thirty-seven influential journals it went, to use Mr. Morrow's own expression, right round the globe.

Chapter VI

A WEEK later, early in May, my glorified friend came up to town, where, it may be veraciously recorded he was the king of the beasts of the year. No advancement was ever more rapid, no exaltation more complete, no bewilderment more teachable. His book sold but moderately, though the article in THE EMPIRE had done unwonted wonders for it; but he circulated in person to a measure that the libraries might well have envied. His formula had been found - he was a "revelation." His momentary terror had been real, just as mine had been - the overclouding of his passionate desire to be left to finish his work. He was far from unsociable, but he had the finest conception of being let alone that I've ever met. For the time, none the less, he took his profit where it seemed most to crowd on him, having in his pocket the portable sophistries about the nature of the artist's task. Observation too was a kind of work and experience a kind of success; London dinners were all material and London ladies were fruitful toil. "No one has the faintest conception of what I'm trying for," he said to me, "and not many have read three pages that I've written; but I must dine with them first - they'll find out why when they've time." It was rather rude justice perhaps; but the fatigue had the merit of being a new sort, while the phantasmagoric town was probably after all less of a battlefield than the haunted study. He once told me that he had had no personal life to speak of since his fortieth year, but had had more than was good for him before. London closed the parenthesis and exhibited him in relations; one of the most inevitable of these being that in which he found himself to Mrs. Weeks Wimbush, wife of the boundless brewer and proprietress of the universal menagerie. In this establishment, as everybody knows, on occasions when the crush is great, the animals rub shoulders freely with the spectators and the lions sit down for whole evenings with the lambs.

It had been ominously clear to me from the first that in Neil Paraday this lady, who, as all the world agreed, was tremendous fun, considered that she had secured a prime attraction, a creature of almost heraldic oddity. Nothing could exceed her enthusiasm over her capture, and nothing could exceed the confused apprehensions it excited in me. I had an instinctive fear of her which I tried without effect to conceal from her victim, but which I let her notice with perfect impunity. Paraday heeded it, but she never did, for her conscience was that of a romping child. She was a blind violent force to which I could attach no more idea of responsibility than to the creaking of a sign in the wind. It was difficult to say what she conduced to but circulation. She was constructed of steel and leather, and all I asked of her for our tractable friend was not to do him to death. He had consented for a time to be of india-rubber, but my thoughts were fixed on the day he should resume his shape or at least get back into his box. It was evidently all right, but I should be glad when it was well over. I had a special fear - the impression was ineffaceable of the hour when, after Mr. Morrow's departure, I had found him on the sofa in his study. That pretext of indisposition had not in the least been meant as a snub to the envoy of THE TATLER - he had gone to lie down in very truth. He had felt a pang of his old pain, the result of the agitation wrought in him by this forcing open of a new period. His old programme, his old ideal even had to be changed. Say what one would, success was a complication and recognition had to be reciprocal. The monastic life, the pious illumination of the missal in the convent cell were things of the gathered past. It didn't engender despair, but at least it required adjustment. Before I left him on that occasion we had passed a bargain, my part of which was that I should make it my business to take care of him. Let whoever would represent the interest in his presence (I must have had a mystical prevision of Mrs. Weeks Wimbush) I should represent the interest in his work - or otherwise expressed in his absence. These two interests were in their essence opposed; and I doubt, as youth is fleeting, if I shall ever again know the intensity of joy with which I felt that in so good a cause I was willing to make myself odious.

One day in Sloane Street I found myself questioning Paraday's landlord, who had come to the door in answer to my knock. Two vehicles, a barouche and a smart hansom, were drawn up before the house.

"In the drawing-room, sir? Mrs. Weeks Wimbush."

"And in the dining-room?"

"A young lady, sir - waiting: I think a foreigner."

It was three o'clock, and on days when Paraday didn't lunch out he attached a value to these appropriated hours. On which days, however, didn't the dear man lunch out? Mrs. Wimbush, at such a crisis, would have rushed round immediately after her own repast. I went into the dining-room first, postponing the pleasure of seeing how, upstairs, the lady of the barouche would, on my arrival, point the moral of my sweet solicitude. No one took such an interest as herself in his doing only what was good for him, and she was always on the spot to see that he did it. She made appointments with him to discuss the best means of economising his time and protecting his privacy. She further made his health her special business, and had so much sympathy with my own zeal for it that she was the author of pleasing fictions on the subject of what my devotion had led me to give up. I gave up nothing (I don't count Mr. Pinhorn) because I had nothing, and all I had as yet achieved was to find myself also in the menagerie. I had dashed in to save my friend, but I had only got domesticated and wedged; so that I could do little more for him than exchange with him over people's heads looks of intense but futile intelligence.

Chapter VII

THE young lady in the dining-room had a brave face, black hair, blue eyes, and in her lap a big volume. "I've come for his autograph," she said when I had explained to her that I was under bonds to see people for him when he was occupied. "I've been waiting half an hour, but I'm prepared to wait all day." I don't know whether it was this that told me she was American, for the propensity to wait all day is not in general characteristic of her race. I was enlightened probably not so much by the spirit of the utterance as by some quality of its sound. At any rate I saw she had an individual patience and a lovely frock, together with an expression that played among her pretty features like a breeze among flowers. Putting her book on the table she showed me a massive album, showily bound and full of autographs of price. The collection of faded notes, of still more faded "thoughts," of quotations, platitudes, signatures, represented a formidable purpose.

I could only disclose my dread of it. "Most people apply to Mr. Paraday by letter, you know."

"Yes, but he doesn't answer. I've written three times."

"Very true," I reflected; "the sort of letter you mean goes straight into the fire."

"How do you know the sort I mean?" My interlocutress had blushed and smiled, and in a moment she added: "I don't believe he gets many like them!"

"I'm sure they're beautiful, but he burns without reading." I didn't add that I had convinced him he ought to.

"Isn't he then in danger of burning things of importance?"

"He would perhaps be so if distinguished men hadn't an infallible nose for nonsense."

She looked at me a moment - her face was sweet and gay. "Do YOU burn without reading too?" - in answer to which I assured her that if she'd trust me with her repository I'd see that Mr. Paraday should write his name in it.

She considered a little. "That's very well, but it wouldn't make me see him."

"Do you want very much to see him?" It seemed ungracious to catechise so charming a creature, but somehow I had never yet taken my duty to the great author so seriously.

"Enough to have come from America for the purpose."

I stared. "All alone?"

"I don't see that that's exactly your business, but if it will make me more seductive I'll confess that I'm quite by myself. I had to come alone or not come at all."

She was interesting; I could imagine she had lost parents, natural protectors - could conceive even she had inherited money. I was at a pass of my own fortunes when keeping hansoms at doors seemed to me pure swagger. As a trick of this bold and sensitive girl, however, it became romantic - a part of the general romance of her freedom, her errand, her innocence. The confidence of young Americans was notorious, and I speedily arrived at a conviction that no impulse could have been more generous than the impulse that had operated here. I foresaw at that moment that it would make her my peculiar charge, just as circumstances had made Neil Paraday. She would be another person to look after, so that one's honour would be concerned in guiding her straight. These things became clearer to me later on; at the instant I had scepticism enough to observe to her, as I turned the pages of her volume, that her net had all the same caught many a big fish. She appeared to have had fruitful access to the great ones of the earth; there were people moreover whose signatures she had presumably secured without a personal interview. She couldn't have worried George Washington and Friedrich Schiller and Hannah More. She met this argument, to my surprise, by throwing up the album without a pang. It wasn't even her own; she was responsible for none of its treasures. It belonged to a girl-friend in America, a young lady in a western city. This young lady had insisted on her bringing it, to pick up more autographs: she thought they might like to see, in Europe, in what company they would be. The "girl-friend," the western city, the immortal names, the curious errand, the idyllic faith, all made a story as strange to me, and as beguiling, as some tale in the Arabian Nights. Thus it was that my informant had encumbered herself with the ponderous tome; but she hastened to assure me that this was the first time she had brought it out. For her visit to Mr. Paraday it had simply been a pretext. She didn't really care a straw that he should write his name; what she did want was to look straight into his face.

I demurred a little. "And why do you require to do that?"

"Because I just love him!" Before I could recover from the agitating effect of this crystal ring my companion had continued:

"Hasn't there ever been any face that you've wanted to look into?"

How could I tell her so soon how much I appreciated the opportunity of looking into hers? I could only assent in general to the proposition that there were certainly for every one such yearnings, and even such faces; and I felt the crisis demand all my lucidity, all my wisdom. "Oh yes, I'm a student of physiognomy. Do you mean," I pursued, "that you've a passion for Mr. Paraday's books?"

"They've been everything to me and a little more beside - I know them by heart. They've completely taken hold of me. There's no author about whom I'm in such a state as I'm in about Neil Paraday."

"Permit me to remark then," I presently returned, "that you're one of the right sort."

"One of the enthusiasts? Of course I am!"

"Oh there are enthusiasts who are quite of the wrong. I mean you're one of those to whom an appeal can be made."

"An appeal?" Her face lighted as if with the chance of some great sacrifice.

If she was ready for one it was only waiting for her, and in a moment I mentioned it. "Give up this crude purpose of seeing him! Go away without it. That will be far better."

She looked mystified, then turned visibly pale. "Why, hasn't he any personal charm?" The girl was terrible and laughable in her bright directness.

"Ah that dreadful word 'personally'!" I wailed; "we're dying of it, for you women bring it out with murderous effect. When you meet with a genius as fine as this idol of ours let him off the dreary duty of being a personality as well. Know him only by what's best in him and spare him for the same sweet sake."

My young lady continued to look at me in confusion and mistrust, and the result of her reflexion on what I had just said was to make her suddenly break out: "Look here, sir - what's the matter with him?"

"The matter with him is that if he doesn't look out people will eat a great hole in his life."

She turned it over. "He hasn't any disfigurement?"

"Nothing to speak of!"

"Do you mean that social engagements interfere with his occupations?"

"That but feebly expresses it."

"So that he can't give himself up to his beautiful imagination?"

"He's beset, badgered, bothered - he's pulled to pieces on the pretext of being applauded. People expect him to give them his time, his golden time, who wouldn't themselves give five shillings for one of his books."

"Five? I'd give five thousand!"

"Give your sympathy - give your forbearance. Two-thirds of those who approach him only do it to advertise themselves."

"Why it's too bad!" the girl exclaimed with the face of an angel.

"It's the first time I was ever called crude!" she laughed.

I followed up my advantage. "There's a lady with him now who's a terrible complication, and who yet hasn't read, I'm sure, ten pages he ever wrote."

My visitor's wide eyes grew tenderer. "Then how does she talk - ?"

"Without ceasing. I only mention her as a single case. Do you want to know how to show a superlative consideration? Simply avoid him."

"Avoid him?" she despairingly breathed.

"Don't force him to have to take account of you; admire him in silence, cultivate him at a distance and secretly appropriate his message. Do you want to know," I continued, warming to my idea, "how to perform an act of homage really sublime?" Then as she hung on my words: "Succeed in never seeing him at all!"

"Never at all?" - she suppressed a shriek for it.

"The more you get into his writings the less you'll want to, and you'll be immensely sustained by the thought of the good you're doing him."

She looked at me without resentment or spite, and at the truth I had put before her with candour, credulity, pity. I was afterwards happy to remember that she must have gathered from my face the liveliness of my interest in herself. "I think I see what you mean."

"Oh I express it badly, but I should be delighted if you'd let me come to see you - to explain it better."

She made no response to this, and her thoughtful eyes fell on the big album, on which she presently laid her hands as if to take it away. "I did use to say out West that they might write a little less for autographs - to all the great poets, you know - and study the thoughts and style a little more."

"What do they care for the thoughts and style? They didn't even understand you. I'm not sure," I added, "that I do myself, and I dare say that you by no means make me out."

She had got up to go, and though I wanted her to succeed in not seeing Neil Paraday I wanted her also, inconsequently, to remain in the house. I was at any rate far from desiring to hustle her off. As Mrs. Weeks Wimbush, upstairs, was still saving our friend in her own way, I asked my young lady to let me briefly relate, in illustration of my point, the little incident of my having gone down into the country for a profane purpose and been converted on the spot to holiness. Sinking again into her chair to listen she showed a deep interest in the anecdote. Then thinking it over gravely she returned with her odd intonation: "Yes, but you do see him!" I had to admit that this was the case; and I wasn't so prepared with an effective attenuation as I could have wished. She eased the situation off, however, by the charming quaintness with which she finally said: "Well, I wouldn't want him to be lonely!" This time she rose in earnest, but I persuaded her to let me keep the album to show Mr. Paraday. I assured her I'd bring it back to her myself. "Well, you'll find my address somewhere in it on a paper!" she sighed all resignedly at the door.

Chapter VIII

I BLUSH to confess it, but I invited Mr. Paraday that very day to transcribe into the album one of his most characteristic passages. I told him how I had got rid of the strange girl who had brought it - her ominous name was Miss Hurter and she lived at an hotel; quite agreeing with him moreover as to the wisdom of getting rid with equal promptitude of the book itself. This was why I carried it to Albemarle Street no later than on the morrow. I failed to find her at home, but she wrote to me and I went again; she wanted so much to hear more about Neil Paraday. I returned repeatedly, I may briefly declare, to supply her with this information. She had been immensely taken, the more she thought of it, with that idea of mine about the act of homage: it had ended by filling her with a generous rapture. She positively desired to do something sublime for him, though indeed I could see that, as this particular flight was difficult, she appreciated the fact that my visits kept her up. I had it on my conscience to keep her up: I neglected nothing that would contribute to it, and her conception of our cherished author's independence became at last as fine as his very own. "Read him, read him - THAT will be an education in decency," I constantly repeated; while, seeking him in his works even as God in nature, she represented herself as convinced that, according to my assurance, this was the system that had, as she expressed it, weaned her. We read him together when I could find time, and the generous creature's sacrifice was fed by our communion. There were twenty selfish women about whom I told her and who stirred her to a beautiful rage. Immediately after my first visit her sister, Mrs. Milsom, came over from Paris, and the two ladies began to present, as they called it, their letters. I thanked our stars that none had been presented to Mr. Paraday. They received invitations and dined out, and some of these occasions enabled Fanny Hurter to perform, for consistency's sake, touching feats of submission. Nothing indeed would now have induced her even to look at the object of her admiration. Once, hearing his name announced at a party, she instantly left the room by another door and then straightway quitted the house. At another time when I was at the opera with them - Mrs. Milsom had invited me to their box - I attempted to point Mr. Paraday out to her in the stalls. On this she asked her sister to change places with her and, while that lady devoured the great man through a powerful glass, presented, all the rest of the evening, her inspired back to the house. To torment her tenderly I pressed the glass upon her, telling her how wonderfully near it brought our friend's handsome head. By way of answer she simply looked at me in charged silence, letting me see that tears had gathered in her eyes. These tears, I may remark, produced an effect on me of which the end is not yet. There was a moment when I felt it my duty to mention them to Neil Paraday, but I was deterred by the reflexion that there were questions more relevant to his happiness.

These question indeed, by the end of the season, were reduced to a single one - the question of reconstituting so far as might be possible the conditions under which he had produced his best work. Such conditions could never all come back, for there was a new one that took up too much place; but some perhaps were not beyond recall. I wanted above all things to see him sit down to the subject he had, on my making his acquaintance, read me that admirable sketch of. Something told me there was no security but in his doing so before the new factor, as we used to say at Mr. Pinhorn's, should render the problem incalculable. It only half-reassured me that the sketch itself was so copious and so eloquent that even at the worst there would be the making of a small but complete book, a tiny volume which, for the faithful, might well become an object of adoration. There would even not be wanting critics to declare, I foresaw, that the plan was a thing to be more thankful for than the structure to have been reared on it. My impatience for the structure, none the less, grew and grew with the interruptions. He had on coming up to town begun to sit for his portrait to a young painter, Mr. Rumble, whose little game, as we also used to say at Mr. Pinhorn's, was to be the first to perch on the shoulders of renown. Mr. Rumble's studio was a circus in which the man of the hour, and still more the woman, leaped through the hoops of his showy frames almost as electrically as they burst into telegrams and "specials." He pranced into the exhibitions on their back; he was the reporter on canvas, the Vandyke up to date, and there was one roaring year in which Mrs. Bounder and Miss Braby, Guy Walsingham and Dora Forbes proclaimed in chorus from the same pictured walls that no one had yet got ahead of him.

Paraday had been promptly caught and saddled, accepting with characteristic good-humour his confidential hint that to figure in his show was not so much a consequence as a cause of immortality. From Mrs. Wimbush to the last "representative" who called to ascertain his twelve favourite dishes, it was the same ingenuous assumption that he would rejoice in the repercussion. There were moments when I fancied I might have had more patience with them if they hadn't been so fatally benevolent. I hated at all events Mr. Rumble's picture, and had my bottled resentment ready when, later on, I found my distracted friend had been stuffed by Mrs. Wimbush into the mouth of another cannon. A young artist in whom she was intensely interested, and who had no connexion with Mr. Rumble, was to show how far he could make him go. Poor Paraday, in return, was naturally to write something somewhere about the young artist. She played her victims against each other with admirable ingenuity, and her establishment was a huge machine in which the tiniest and the biggest wheels went round to the same treadle. I had a scene with her in which I tried to express that the function of such a man was to exercise his genius - not to serve as a hoarding for pictorial posters. The people I was perhaps angriest with were the editors of magazines who had introduced what they called new features, so aware were they that the newest feature of all would be to make him grind their axes by contributing his views on vital topics and taking part in the periodical prattle about the future of fiction. I made sure that before I should have done with him there would scarcely be a current form of words left me to be sick of; but meanwhile I could make surer still of my animosity to bustling ladies for whom he drew the water that irrigated their social flower-beds.

I had a battle with Mrs. Wimbush over the artist she protected, and another over the question of a certain week, at the end of July, that Mr. Paraday appeared to have contracted to spend with her in the country. I protested against this visit; I intimated that he was too unwell for hospitality without a nuance, for caresses without imagination; I begged he might rather take the time in some restorative way. A sultry air of promises, of ponderous parties, hung over his August, and he would greatly profit by the interval of rest. He hadn't told me he was ill again that he had had a warning; but I hadn't needed this, for I found his reticence his worst symptom. The only thing he said to me was that he believed a comfortable attack of something or other would set him up: it would put out of the question everything but the exemptions he prized. I'm afraid I shall have presented him as a martyr in a very small cause if I fail to explain that he surrendered himself much more liberally than I surrendered him. He filled his lungs, for the most part; with the comedy of his queer fate: the tragedy was in the spectacles through which I chose to look. He was conscious of inconvenience, and above all of a great renouncement; but how could he have heard a mere dirge in the bells of his accession? The sagacity and the jealousy were mine, and his the impressions and the harvest. Of course, as regards Mrs. Wimbush, I was worsted in my encounters, for wasn't the state of his health the very reason for his coming to her at Prestidge? Wasn't it precisely at Prestidge that he was to be coddled, and wasn't the dear Princess coming to help her to coddle him? The dear Princess, now on a visit to England, was of a famous foreign house, and, in her gilded cage, with her retinue of keepers and feeders, was the most expensive specimen in the good lady's collection. I don't think her august presence had had to do with Paraday's consenting to go, but it's not impossible he had operated as a bait to the illustrious stranger. The party had been made up for him, Mrs. Wimbush averred, and every one was counting on it, the dear Princess most of all. If he was well enough he was to read them something absolutely fresh, and it was on that particular prospect the Princess had set her heart. She was so fond of genius in ANY walk of life, and was so used to it and understood it so well: she was the greatest of Mr. Paraday's admirers, she devoured everything he wrote. And then he read like an angel. Mrs. Wimbush reminded me that he had again and again given her, Mrs. Wimbush, the privilege of listening to him.

I looked at her a moment. "What has he read to you?" I crudely enquired.

For a moment too she met my eyes, and for the fraction of a moment she hesitated and coloured. "Oh all sorts of things!"

I wondered if this were an imperfect recollection or only a perfect fib, and she quite understood my unuttered comment on her measure of such things. But if she could forget Neil Paraday's beauties she could of course forget my rudeness, and three days later she invited me, by telegraph, to join the party at Prestidge. This time she might indeed have had a story about what I had given up to be near the master. I addressed from that fine residence several communications to a young lady in London, a young lady whom, I confess, I quitted with reluctance and whom the reminder of what she herself could give up was required to make me quit at all. It adds to the gratitude I owe her on other grounds that she kindly allows me to transcribe from my letters a few of the passages in which that hateful sojourn is candidly commemorated.

Chapter IX

"I SUPPOSE I ought to enjoy the joke of what's going on here," I wrote, "but somehow it doesn't amuse me. Pessimism on the contrary possesses me and cynicism deeply engages. I positively feel my own flesh sore from the brass nails in Neil Paraday's social harness. The house is full of people who like him, as they mention, awfully, and with whom his talent for talking nonsense has prodigious success. I delight in his nonsense myself; why is it therefore that I grudge these happy folk their artless satisfaction? Mystery of the human heart - abyss of the critical spirit! Mrs. Wimbush thinks she can answer that question, and as my want of gaiety has at last worn out her patience she has given me a glimpse of her shrewd guess. I'm made restless by the selfishness of the insincere friend - I want to monopolise Paraday in order that he may push me on. To be intimate with him is a feather in my cap; it gives me an importance that I couldn't naturally pretend to, and I seek to deprive him of social refreshment because I fear that meeting more disinterested people may enlighten him as to my real motive. All the disinterested people here are his particular admirers and have been carefully selected as such. There's supposed to be a copy of his last book in the house, and in the hall I come upon ladies, in attitudes, bending gracefully over the first volume. I discreetly avert my eyes, and when I next look round the precarious joy has been superseded by the book of life. There's a sociable circle or a confidential couple, and the relinquished volume lies open on its face and as dropped under extreme coercion. Somebody else presently finds it and transfers it, with its air of momentary desolation, to another piece of furniture. Every one's asking every one about it all day, and every one's telling every one where they put it last. I'm sure it's rather smudgy about the twentieth page. I've a strong impression, too, that the second volume is lost - has been packed in the bag of some departing guest; and yet everybody has the impression that somebody else has read to the end. You see therefore that the beautiful book plays a great part in our existence. Why should I take the occasion of such distinguished honours to say that I begin to see deeper into Gustave Flaubert's doleful refrain about the hatred of literature? I refer you again to the perverse constitution of man.

"The Princess is a massive lady with the organisation of an athlete and the confusion of tongues of a valet de place. She contrives to commit herself extraordinarily little in a great many languages, and is entertained and conversed with in detachments and relays, like an institution which goes on from generation to generation or a big building contracted for under a forfeit. She can't have a personal taste any more than, when her husband succeeds, she can have a personal crown, and her opinion on any matter is rusty and heavy and plain - made, in the night of ages, to last and be transmitted. I feel as if I ought to 'tip' some custode for my glimpse of it. She has been told everything in the world and has never perceived anything, and the echoes of her education respond awfully to the rash footfall - I mean the casual remark - in the cold Valhalla of her memory. Mrs. Wimbush delights in her wit and says there's nothing so charming as to hear Mr. Paraday draw it out. He's perpetually detailed for this job, and he tells me it has a peculiarly exhausting effect. Every one's beginning - at the end of two days - to sidle obsequiously away from her, and Mrs. Wimbush pushes him again and again into the breach. None of the uses I have yet seen him put to infuriate me quite so much. He looks very fagged and has at last confessed to me that his condition makes him uneasy - has even promised me he'll go straight home instead of returning to his final engagements in town. Last night I had some talk with him about going to-day, cutting his visit short; so sure am I that he'll be better as soon as he's shut up in his lighthouse. He told me that this is what he would like to do; reminding me, however, that the first lesson of his greatness has been precisely that he can't do what he likes. Mrs. Wimbush would never forgive him if he should leave her before the Princess has received the last hand. When I hint that a violent rupture with our hostess would be the best thing in the world for him he gives me to understand that if his reason assents to the proposition his courage hangs woefully back. He makes no secret of being mortally afraid of her, and when I ask what harm she can do him that she hasn't already done he simply repeats: 'I'm afraid, I'm afraid! Don't enquire too closely,' he said last night; 'only believe that I feel a sort of terror. It's strange, when she's so kind! At any rate, I'd as soon overturn that piece of priceless Sevres as tell her I must go before my date.' It sounds dreadfully weak, but he has some reason, and he pays for his imagination, which puts him (I should hate it) in the place of others and makes him feel, even against himself, their feelings, their appetites, their motives. It's indeed inveterately against himself that he makes his imagination act. What a pity he has such a lot of it! He's too beastly intelligent. Besides, the famous reading's still to come off, and it has been postponed a day to allow Guy Walsingham to arrive. It appears this eminent lady's staying at a house a few miles off, which means of course that Mrs. Wimbush has forcibly annexed her. She's to come over in a day or two - Mrs. Wimbush wants her to hear Mr. Paraday.

"To-day's wet and cold, and several of the company, at the invitation of the Duke, have driven over to luncheon at Bigwood. I saw poor Paraday wedge himself, by command, into the little supplementary seat of a brougham In which the Princess and our hostess were already ensconced. If the front glass isn't open on his dear old back perhaps he'll survive. Bigwood, I believe, is very grand and frigid, all marble and precedence, and I wish him well out of the adventure. I can't tell you how much more and more your attitude to him, in the midst of all this, shines out by contrast. I never willingly talk to these people about him, but see what a comfort I find it to scribble to you! I appreciate it - it keeps me warm; there are no fires in the house. Mrs. Wimbush goes by the calendar, the temperature goes by the weather, the weather goes by God knows what, and the Princess is easily heated. I've nothing but my acrimony to warm me, and have been out under an umbrella to restore my circulation. Coming in an hour ago I found Lady Augusta Minch rummaging about the hall. When I asked her what she was looking for she said she had mislaid something that Mr. Paraday had lent her. I ascertained in a moment that the article in question is a manuscript, and I've a foreboding that it's the noble morsel he read me six weeks ago. When I expressed my surprise that he should have bandied about anything so precious (I happen to know it's his only copy - in the most beautiful hand in all the world) Lady Augusta confessed to me that she hadn't had it from himself, but from Mrs. Wimbush, who had wished to give her a glimpse of it as a salve for her not being able to stay and hear it read.

"'Is that the piece he's to read,' I asked, 'when Guy Walsingham arrives?'

"'It's not for Guy Walsingham they're waiting now, it's for Dora Forbes,' Lady Augusta said. 'She's coming, I believe, early to-morrow. Meanwhile Mrs. Wimbush has found out about him, and is actively wiring to him. She says he also must hear him.'

"'You bewilder me a little,' I replied; 'in the age we live in one gets lost among the genders and the pronouns. The clear thing is that Mrs. Wimbush doesn't guard such a treasure so jealously as she might.'

"'Poor dear, she has the Princess to guard! Mr. Paraday lent her the manuscript to look over.'

"'She spoke, you mean, as if it were the morning paper?'

"Lady Augusta stared - my irony was lost on her. 'She didn't have time, so she gave me a chance first; because unfortunately I go to-morrow to Bigwood.'

"'And your chance has only proved a chance to lose it?'

"'I haven't lost it. I remember now - it was very stupid of me to have forgotten. I told my maid to give it to Lord Dorimont - or at least to his man.'

"'And Lord Dorimont went away directly after luncheon.'

"'Of course he gave it back to my maid - or else his man did,' said Lady Augusta. 'I dare say it's all right.'

"The conscience of these people is like a summer sea. They haven't time to look over a priceless composition; they've only time to kick it about the house. I suggested that the 'man,' fired with a noble emulation, had perhaps kept the work for his own perusal; and her ladyship wanted to know whether, if the thing shouldn't reappear for the grand occasion appointed by our hostess, the author wouldn't have something else to read that would do just as well. Their questions are too delightful! I declared to Lady Augusta briefly that nothing in the world can ever do so well as the thing that does best; and at this she looked a little disconcerted. But I added that if the manuscript had gone astray our little circle would have the less of an effort of attention to make. The piece in question was very long - it would keep them three hours.

"'Three hours! Oh the Princess will get up!' said Lady Augusta.

"'I thought she was Mr. Paraday's greatest admirer.'

"'I dare say she is - she's so awfully clever. But what's the use of being a Princess -'

"'If you can't dissemble your love?' I asked as Lady Augusta was vague. She said at any rate she'd question her maid; and I'm hoping that when I go down to dinner I shall find the manuscript has been recovered."

Chapter X

"IT has NOT been recovered," I wrote early the next day, "and I'm moreover much troubled about our friend. He came back from Bigwood with a chill and, being allowed to have a fire in his room, lay down a while before dinner. I tried to send him to bed and indeed thought I had put him in the way of it; but after I had gone to dress Mrs. Wimbush came up to see him, with the inevitable result that when I returned I found him under arms and flushed and feverish, though decorated with the rare flower she had brought him for his button-hole. He came down to dinner, but Lady Augusta Minch was very shy of him. To-day he's in great pain, and the advent of ces dames - I mean of Guy Walsingham and Dora Forbes - doesn't at all console me. It does Mrs. Wimbush, however, for she has consented to his remaining in bed so that he may be all right to-morrow for the listening circle. Guy Walsingham's already on the scene, and the Doctor for Paraday also arrived early. I haven't yet seen the author of 'Obsessions,' but of course I've had a moment by myself with the Doctor. I tried to get him to say that our invalid must go straight home - I mean to-morrow or next day; but he quite refuses to talk about the future. Absolute quiet and warmth and the regular administration of an important remedy are the points he mainly insists on. He returns this afternoon, and I'm to go back to see the patient at one o'clock, when he next takes his medicine. It consoles me a little that he certainly won't be able to read - an exertion he was already more than unfit for. Lady Augusta went off after breakfast, assuring me her first care would be to follow up the lost manuscript. I can see she thinks me a shocking busybody and doesn't understand my alarm, but she'll do what she can, for she's a good-natured woman. 'So are they all honourable men.' That was precisely what made her give the thing to Lord Dorimont and made Lord Dorimont bag it. What use HE has for it God only knows. I've the worst forebodings, but somehow I'm strangely without passion - desperately calm. As I consider the unconscious, the well-meaning ravages of our appreciative circle I bow my head in submission to some great natural, some universal accident; I'm rendered almost indifferent, in fact quite gay (ha-ha!) by the sense of immitigable fate. Lady Augusta promises me to trace the precious object and let me have it through the post by the time Paraday's well enough to play his part with it. The last evidence is that her maid did give it to his lordship's valet. One would suppose it some thrilling number of THE FAMILY BUDGET. Mrs. Wimbush, who's aware of the accident, is much less agitated by it than she would doubtless be were she not for the hour inevitably engrossed with Guy Walsingham."

Later in the day I informed my correspondent, for whom indeed I kept a loose diary of the situation, that I had made the acquaintance of this celebrity and that she was a pretty little girl who wore her hair in what used to be called a crop. She looked so juvenile and so innocent that if, as Mr. Morrow had announced, she was resigned to the larger latitude, her superiority to prejudice must have come to her early. I spent most of the day hovering about Neil Paraday's room, but it was communicated to me from below that Guy Walsingham, at Prestidge, was a success. Toward evening I became conscious somehow that her superiority was contagious, and by the time the company separated for the night I was sure the larger latitude had been generally accepted. I thought of Dora Forbes and felt that he had no time to lose. Before dinner I received a telegram from Lady Augusta Minch. "Lord Dorimont thinks he must have left bundle in train - enquire." How could I enquire - if I was to take the word as a command? I was too worried and now too alarmed about Neil Paraday. The Doctor came back, and it was an immense satisfaction to me to be sure he was wise and interested. He was proud of being called to so distinguished a patient, but he admitted to me that night that my friend was gravely ill. It was really a relapse, a recrudescence of his old malady. There could be no question of moving him: we must at any rate see first, on the spot, what turn his condition would take. Meanwhile, on the morrow, he was to have a nurse. On the morrow the dear man was easier, and my spirits rose to such cheerfulness that I could almost laugh over Lady Augusta's second telegram: "Lord Dorimont's servant been to station - nothing found. Push enquiries." I did laugh, I'm sure, as I remembered this to be the mystic scroll I had scarcely allowed poor Mr. Morrow to point his umbrella at. Fool that I had been: the thirty-seven influential journals wouldn't have destroyed it, they'd only have printed it. Of course I said nothing to Paraday.

When the nurse arrived she turned me out of the room, on which I went downstairs. I should premise that at breakfast the news that our brilliant friend was doing well excited universal complacency, and the Princess graciously remarked that he was only to be commiserated for missing the society of Miss Collop. Mrs. Wimbush, whose social gift never shone brighter than in the dry decorum with which she accepted this fizzle in her fireworks, mentioned to me that Guy Walsingham had made a very favourable impression on her Imperial Highness. Indeed I think every one did so, and that, like the money-market or the national honour, her Imperial Highness was constitutionally sensitive. There was a certain gladness, a perceptible bustle in the air, however, which I thought slightly anomalous in a house where a great author lay critically ill. "Le roy est mort - vive le roy": I was reminded that another great author had already stepped into his shoes. When I came down again after the nurse had taken possession I found a strange gentleman hanging about the hall and pacing to and fro by the closed door of the drawing-room. This personage was florid and bald; he had a big red moustache and wore showy knickerbockers - characteristics all that fitted to my conception of the identity of Dora Forbes. In a moment I saw what had happened: the author of "The Other Way Round" had just alighted at the portals of Prestidge, but had suffered a scruple to restrain him from penetrating further. I recognised his scruple when, pausing to listen at his gesture of caution, I heard a shrill voice lifted in a sort of rhythmic uncanny chant. The famous reading had begun, only it was the author of "Obsessions" who now furnished the sacrifice. The new visitor whispered to me that he judged something was going on he oughtn't to interrupt.

"Miss Collop arrived last night," I smiled, "and the Princess has a thirst for the inedit."

Dora Forbes lifted his bushy brows. "Miss Collop?"

"Guy Walsingham, your distinguished confrere - or shall I say your formidable rival?"

"Oh!" growled Dora Forbes. Then he added: "Shall I spoil it if I go in?"

"I should think nothing could spoil it!" I ambiguously laughed.

Dora Forbes evidently felt the dilemma; he gave an irritated crook to his moustache. "SHALL I go in?" he presently asked.

We looked at each other hard a moment; then I expressed something bitter that was in me, expressed it in an infernal "Do!" After this I got out into the air, but not so fast as not to hear, when the door of the drawing-room opened, the disconcerted drop of Miss Collop's public manner: she must have been in the midst of the larger latitude. Producing with extreme rapidity, Guy Walsingham has just published a work in which amiable people who are not initiated have been pained to see the genius of a sister-novelist held up to unmistakeable ridicule; so fresh an exhibition does it seem to them of the dreadful way men have always treated women. Dora Forbes, it's true, at the present hour, is immensely pushed by Mrs. Wimbush and has sat for his portrait to the young artists she protects, sat for it not only in oils but in monumental alabaster.

What happened at Prestidge later in the day is of course contemporary history. If the interruption I had whimsically sanctioned was almost a scandal, what is to be said of that general scatter of the company which, under the Doctor's rule, began to take place in the evening? His rule was soothing to behold, small comfort as I was to have at the end. He decreed in the interest of his patient an absolutely soundless house and a consequent break-up of the party. Little country practitioner as he was, he literally packed off the Princess. She departed as promptly as if a revolution had broken out, and Guy Walsingham emigrated with her. I was kindly permitted to remain, and this was not denied even to Mrs. Wimbush. The privilege was withheld indeed from Dora Forbes; so Mrs. Wimbush kept her latest capture temporarily concealed. This was so little, however, her usual way of dealing with her eminent friends that a couple of days of it exhausted her patience, and she went up to town with him in great publicity. The sudden turn for the worse her afflicted guest had, after a brief improvement, taken on the third night raised an obstacle to her seeing him before her retreat; a fortunate circumstance doubtless, for she was fundamentally disappointed in him. This was not the kind of performance for which she had invited him to Prestidge, let alone invited the Princess. I must add that none of the generous acts marking her patronage of intellectual and other merit have done so much for her reputation as her lending Neil Paraday the most beautiful of her numerous homes to die in. He took advantage to the utmost of the singular favour. Day by day I saw him sink, and I roamed alone about the empty terraces and gardens. His wife never came near him, but I scarcely noticed it: as I paced there with rage in my heart I was too full of another wrong. In the event of his death it would fall to me perhaps to bring out in some charming form, with notes, with the tenderest editorial care, that precious heritage of his written project. But where was that precious heritage and were both the author and the book to have been snatched from us? Lady Augusta wrote me that she had done all she could and that poor Lord Dorimont, who had really been worried to death, was extremely sorry. I couldn't have the matter out with Mrs. Wimbush, for I didn't want to be taunted by her with desiring to aggrandise myself by a public connexion with Mr. Paraday's sweepings. She had signified her willingness to meet the expense of all advertising, as indeed she was always ready to do. The last night of the horrible series, the night before he died, I put my ear closer to his pillow.

"That thing I read you that morning, you know."

"In your garden that dreadful day? Yes!"

"Won't it do as it is?"

"It would have been a glorious book."

"It IS a glorious book," Neil Paraday murmured. "Print it as it stands - beautifully."

"Beautifully!" I passionately promised.

It may be imagined whether, now that he's gone, the promise seems to me less sacred. I'm convinced that if such pages had appeared in his lifetime the Abbey would hold him to-day. I've kept the advertising in my own hands, but the manuscript has not been recovered. It's impossible, and at any rate intolerable, to suppose it can have been wantonly destroyed. Perhaps some hazard of a blind hand, some brutal fatal ignorance has lighted kitchen-fires with it. Every stupid and hideous accident haunts my meditations. My undiscourageable search for the lost treasure would make a long chapter. Fortunately I've a devoted associate in the person of a young lady who has every day a fresh indignation and a fresh idea, and who maintains with intensity that the prize will still turn up. Sometimes I believe her, but I've quite ceased to believe myself. The only thing for us at all events is to go on seeking and hoping together; and we should be closely united by this firm tie even were we not at present by another.

Henry James – A Biography

Henry James (1843-1916) is today remembered as the most prolific American novelist of the late nineteenth century and early twentieth century whose works have become part and parcel of the American literary tradition and of American heritage in general. Having lived most of his life as an expatriate in Europe, many of James's novels juxtapose the Old World with the New World. Novels like *The Portrait of a Lady*, *Daisy Miller* and *The Ambassadors*, among many others, display the encounter between American and European cultures and mentalities. They highlight the differences between the two worlds through following the experiences of American expatriates in Europe. Furthermore, James's fiction also transcends this recurring theme to offer sophisticated observations of human relations as well as realistic, social criticism.

Born on April 15th, 1843, in New York City, Henry James is the son of Henry James, Sr. and the brother of the famous American psychologist and philosopher William James. The father was himself an intellectual and a theologian who had inherited a considerable fortune from his Irish ancestors and who was able to provide his children with necessary conditions for brilliance. A passionate thirst for knowledge and learning was inculcated in the children by the father who, in the mid-1850s, took the family for a tour around the European continent. In Europe, Henry James had private tutors in France, England, Germany, Poland and Switzerland. Later, on their return to America, the family settled in Cambridge, Massachusetts, where they had the opportunity to host famous intellectual and literary figures such as Ralph Waldo Emerson, Henry David Thoreau and Washington Irving.

It was during their first stay in Europe that Henry James became very attached to the old continent. Later, he started by multiplying his visits to England and

France before deciding to settle definitively in London. Unlike his brother William who made an outstanding academic career at Harvard, James did not have a formal education, and even when he joined the Harvard law school, he left it within only one year to concentrate on his writing activities. Henry James was an avid reader and the luxury of his father's household allowed him to nourish his talents. Between 1864 and 1865, he published his first installments in literary magazines with the help of William Dean Howells.

Henry James's first short story, *A Tragedy of Error*, was published in the *Continental Monthly* magazine in 1864. Other publications soon followed in *The Nation* and *Atlantic Monthly*. Later, and after a new tour in Europe, James published his first novel *Watch and Ward* in 1870. Other visits to Europe took place and the publications of new books followed, including *Roderick Hudson*, *A Passionate Pilgrim* and *Transatlantic Sketches*. With these early works, James started to develop the major theme that haunted most of his oeuvre: American innocence and freshness meeting European tradition and experience. In such works, as well as in many other novels by Henry James, the novelist draws on his own experience in Europe and his acquaintances among American expatriates there.

In 1876, realizing that Europe was much more suitable for his career as a writer and as a realistic novelist, James decided to settle in Europe, the land of outstanding contemporaries such as Gustave Flaubert, Emile Zola and Ivan Turgenev. James spent most of his expatriate years around London in addition to Paris and Rome. Other works portraying Americans living in Europe followed, the most successful of which was probably the novella *Daisy Miller* (1879). The book follows the romantic adventures of an innocent American young woman who finds difficulties to adapt to European values and lifestyle. James's *The Portrait of a Lady* (1881) almost deals with the same theme, equally having as a central character an American lady in European distress, though she has to face the Machiavellian enterprises of fellow American expatriates.

Among James's other publications during this period, one can mention *The Europeans*, *Washington Square* and *Confidence*. These were later followed by a social drama entitled *The Bostonians*. In 1988, another seminal novella appeared in *The Atlantic Monthly* entitled *The Aspern Papers*. Though equally set in Europe (Venice, Italy), the novella deals with a different kind of themes. It tells the story of the love letters that a famous and now dead poet had written to his beloved. The poet's beloved, now an aged woman, is visited by the narrator who is secretly after the letters. The narrative is a masterpiece of suspense in addition to its dexterous description of the dreamlike city of Venice.

In the beginning of the 1890s, James was encouraged to enter the world of drama. He converted into theatre some of his fiction such as *The American* and *Daisy Miller*. In late nineteenth-century England and Europe, the stage was a perfect tool to introduce literary works to the large public and to help the author make considerable amounts of money. With Henry James, this worked for a while until 1895 when the negative reaction of the audience at the opening of his play *Guy Domville* made him decide to abandon drama for good. The decision was encouraged by the fact that he had already published quite successful stories during that same period. Indeed, in 1890, James published what many critics believe to be as one of his major masterpieces, *The Tragic Muse*. The latter was followed by another successful short story entitled "The Pupil" (1891). Being first published in *Longman's Magazine*, "The Pupil" tells the story of a young boy named Morgan Moreen and his relationship with his tutor Pemberton. Some critics commented on the homoerotic nature of the relationship between Pemberton and Morgan and even advance the theory that Henry James was himself a homosexual, an idea encouraged by the fact that James was a life-long celibate.

In 1898, while still living in England, James published a collection of short stories entitled *The Two Magics*. It included a number of tales in addition to the two longer stories "Covering End" and "The Turn of the Screw," of which the latter was an outstanding success. "The Turn of the Screw," basically a ghost story, was believed to have a great impact on the genre and on Gothic fiction. James took after his father an interest in spiritual and paranormal phenomena which pushed him to deal with the theme in fiction. The story centers around the character of a late governess who claims to have seen the figures of a man and a woman while they are not seen by others. The events are ambiguous and reality is blurred and confused with pure imagination, which is supposedly the major feature behind the captivating nature of the novella.

Many other works followed, the most important of which was probably *The Ambassadors* (1903) which James himself considered as his finest work. The story of *The Ambassadors* deals again with the theme of Americans visiting Europe. The narrator Lewis Lambert Strether has to go to Paris to look for Chad Newsome, his wealthy fiancée's son. The book mainly deals with the difficulties Lewis is to encounter during his mission in Europe. The old continent is again portrayed as a world of experience and authenticity, but also as a world of corruption and ruination. Mrs. Newsome sends other Americans after Chad and the latter are referred to as "ambassadors."

After decades spent in Europe, Hanry James finally visited his home country between 1904 and 1905 and many other publications followed including "The Jolly Corner" (1908) and *The Outcry* (1911). He also proofread his works for republication and wrote critical prefaces for the New York Edition. In 1911 and then in 1912, James received honorary degrees from Harvard and Oxford respectively. In 1915, one year before his death, Henry James became officially a British citizen, which caused significant disappointment and stimulated contempt among many of his countrymen. James's decision was mainly in reaction to his country's position on the First World War. During this autumnal period of his life, James also finished his two autobiographical works entitled *A Small Boy* and *Notes of a Son and Brother*. On February 28th, 1916, Henry James died after a long illness. While his cremation and funerals took place in London, his ashes were taken to be buried in his American old home at Cambridge, Massachusetts.

During Henry James's lifetime and after his death, his works have been criticized by numerous literary men and critics, including celebrated figures like Oscar Wilde and Virginia Woolf. His fiction has been criticized for its sophistication and elitist nature. In fact, Henry James's works are far from being accessible for everyone. Furthermore, some observers and critics also complain about the fact that James's protagonists always belong to the middle or the upper social class. Unlike the fiction of Charles Dickens or Thomas Hardy, James's stories never concern themselves with the poor and the deprived. On the other hand, most readers and critics agree on the subtlety of James's realism and on his descriptive and narratorial craftsmanship and delicacy. Many of the twenty-two novels and the more than a hundred tales, short stories and travelogues that he wrote have now become landmarks of American literature and heritage.